This Little Tiger book belongs to:

_____

_____

_____

_____

To my friend, Nick

LITTLE TIGER PRESS
An imprint of Magi Publications
1 The Coda Centre, 189 Munster Road, London SW6 6AW
www.littletigerpress.com

First published in Great Britain 2005
This edition published 2005

Text and illustrations copyright © Ruth Galloway 2005
Ruth Galloway has asserted her right to be identified as the author and illustrator of
this work under the Copyright, Designs and Patents Act, 1988
A CIP catalogue record for this book is available from the British Library

Printed in Belgium by Proost NV.

2 4 6 8 10 9 7 5 3

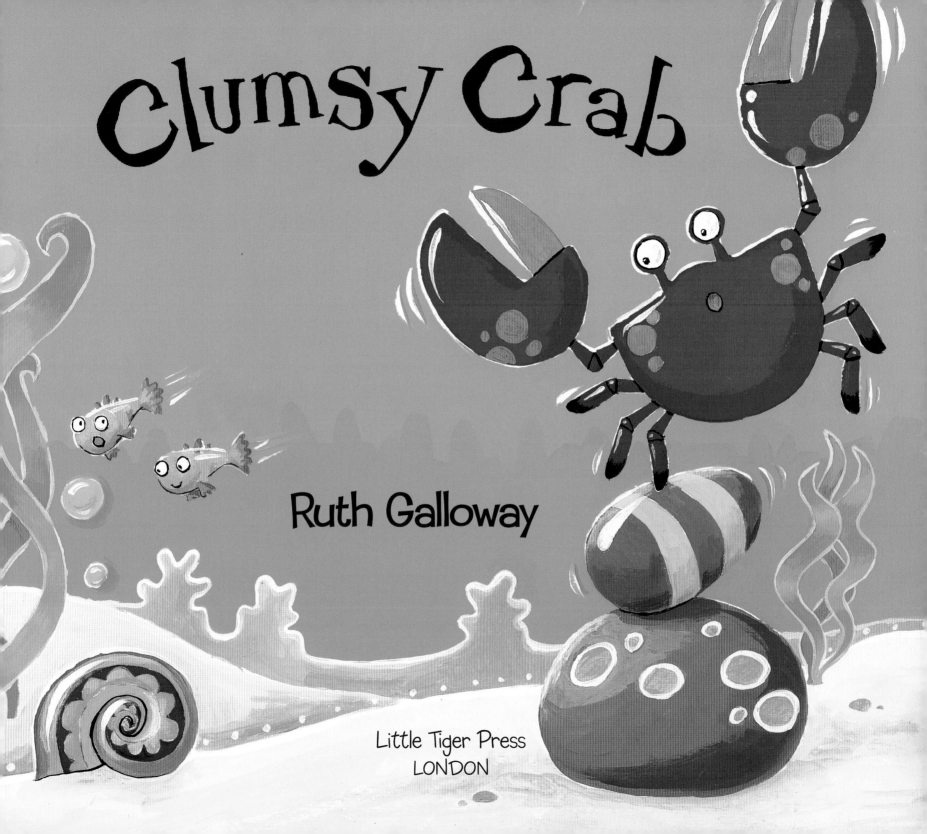

Clumsy Crab

Ruth Galloway

Little Tiger Press
LONDON

Nipper the crab hated his huge clumsy claws. However hard he tried they always got in the way.

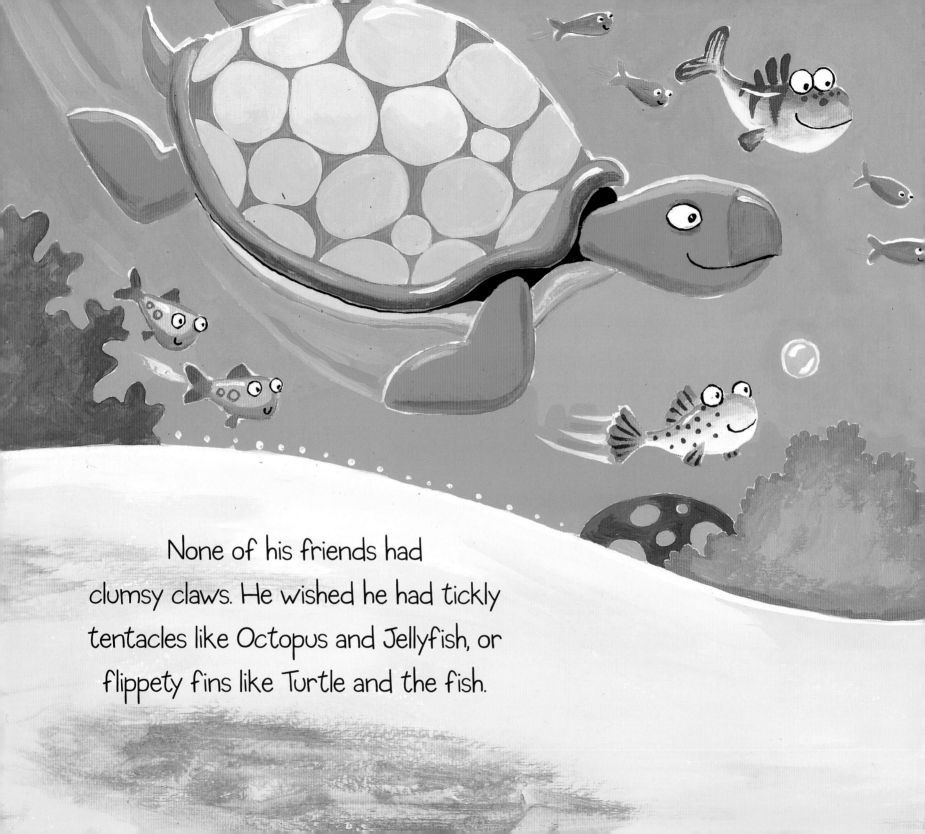

None of his friends had clumsy claws. He wished he had tickly tentacles like Octopus and Jellyfish, or flippety fins like Turtle and the fish.

One day Nipper was playing
catch the bubble with his friends.

They couldn't play
that game any more. They
played chase instead.

Nipper scuttled off sideways,
but one of his clumsy claws got in the way.

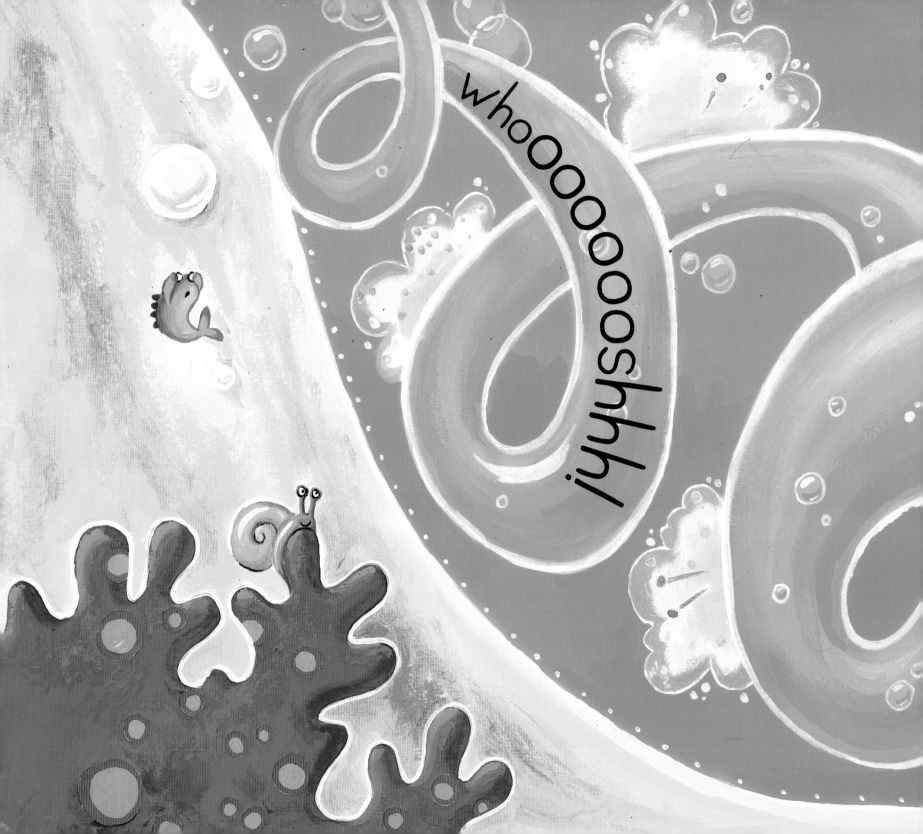

He slipped and stumbled,
tripped and tumbled until . . .

. . . he was buried up to his eyes
in sand. Turtle had to dig him out.

They all decided to play hide and seek. Crab climbed into a big clam shell and pulled it shut.

It was the
PERFECT
hiding place. Until...

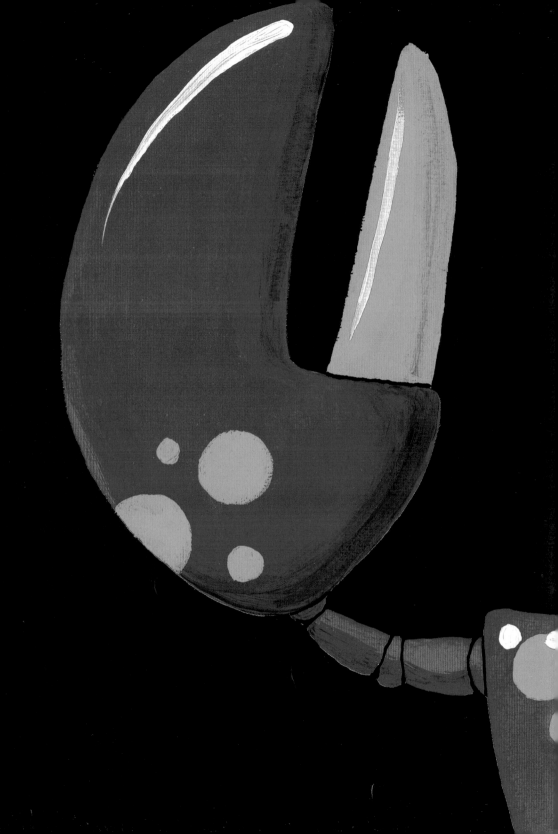

CRACK!

... Nipper's clumsy claws shattered
the shell into hundreds of tiny pieces.
"Ouch!" he cried.

Nipper sighed. "If only I didn't have
these claws I'd be good at hide and seek."
"Don't worry, Nipper," said Jellyfish, picking up the
pieces of shell. "We'll hide, and you can find us."

Nipper counted to ten then set off to find his friends. He searched in the sand . . . and found Turtle.

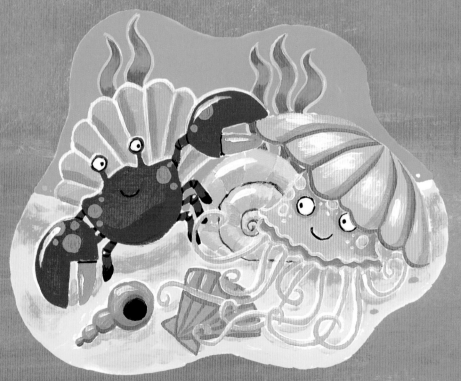

He searched under the shells . . . and found Jellyfish.

He searched up and down and in and out of rocks . . .

but he couldn't find
Octopus anywhere.

Then they heard a cry.
Octopus was tightly tangled
in some seaweed.

Help!

Octopus squirmed and squiggled and wriggled and jiggled. Turtle and Jellyfish tried to help, but the knots just got tighter and tighter.

Nipper had an idea.

He gently snipped at the seaweed with his claws and small pieces floated away. Faster and faster Nipper danced around the clump of seaweed.

His claws moved quickly, slashing and slicing, shredding and dicing, until the sea was filled with pieces of seaweed swirling all around.

Octopus was finally free!
"Thank you, you clever crab!" he cheered.
Nipper waved his claws happily. At last
he knew how useful they could be.

More Little Tiger books to get your claws on

Nobody Laughs at a Lion!

Paul Bright Illustrated by Matt Buckingham

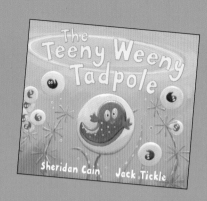

The Teeny Weeny Tadpole

Sheridan Cain   Jack Tickle

Fidgety Fish

Ruth Galloway

Too Busy for Benjie

Christine Leeson
Andy Ellis

What Bear Likes Best!

Alison Ritchie
illustrated by
Dubravka Kolanovic

Claire Freedman and Daniel Howarth

The Busy Busy Day

For information regarding
any of these titles or for
our catalogue, please contact us:
Little Tiger Press, 1 The Coda Centre,
189 Munster Road, London SW6 6AW, UK
Tel: 020 7385 6333 Fax: 020 7385 7333
E-mail: info@littletiger.co.uk www.littletigerpress.com